A Rescue
by Peace and Love

Susan Koch Sheppard

AuthorHouse™
1663 Liberty Drive
Bloomington, IN 47403
www.authorhouse.com
Phone: 1 (833) 262-8899

Because of the dynamic nature of the Internet, any web addresses or links contained in this book may have changed
since publication and may no longer be valid. The views expressed in this work are solely those of the author and do not
necessarily reflect the views of the publisher, and the publisher hereby disclaims any responsibility for them.

Any people depicted in stock imagery provided by Getty Images are models,
and such images are being used for illustrative purposes only.
Certain stock imagery © Getty Images.

This book is printed on acid-free paper.

ISBN: 978-1-7283-7292-1 (sc)
ISBN: 978-1-7283-7294-5 (hc)
ISBN: 978-1-7283-7293-8 (e)

Library of Congress Control Number: 2020917032

Print information available on the last page.

Published by AuthorHouse 09/18/2020

authorHOUSE

This book is dedicated to my daughters, Andrea and Teresa, and my grandson Ian. With additional thanks to Becca, and my sister Sandy for their help with the book. Special thanks to "Shake" for his encouragement.

One summer's day, Peace and Love were passing through the door of their house when they heard a noise from the bush around the corner of the door. Peace said, "What is that?" The noise was a low cooing sound and fluttering of leaves and branches.

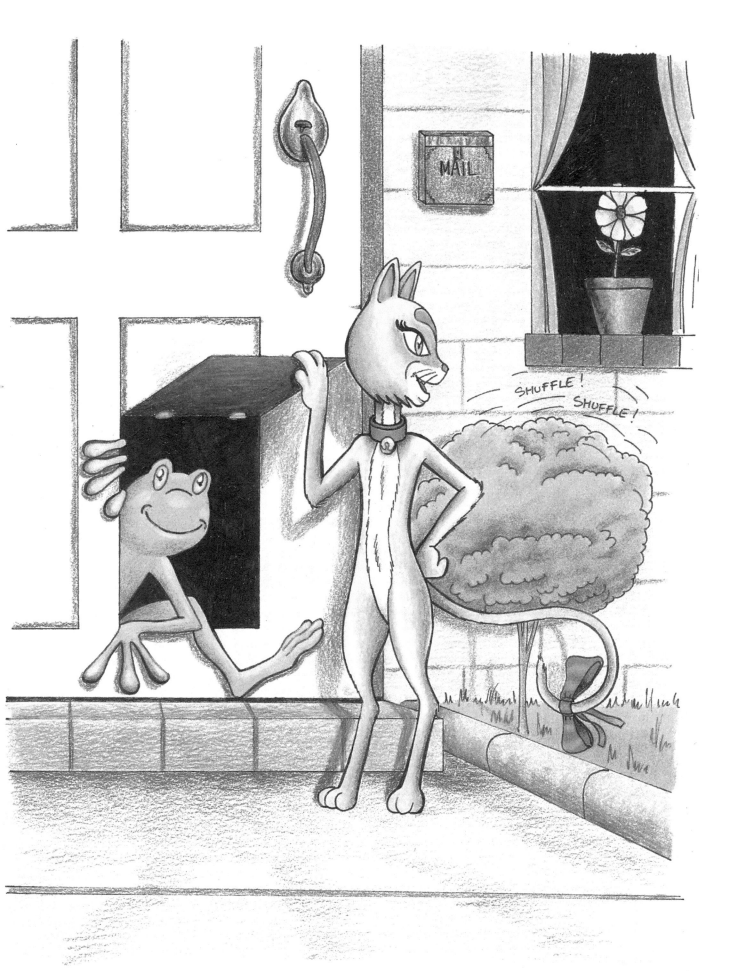

Love went to the bush, pushing in to see, "Peace, look!" she exclaimed.

It was an injured mourning dove, flapping and struggling to move in the bush.

Peace said, "You must get the children. They will help the dove. I will wait here with the dove."

Love re-entered the house, finding the children, Matt and Dawn.

Love meowed with such distress; the children knew something was wrong.

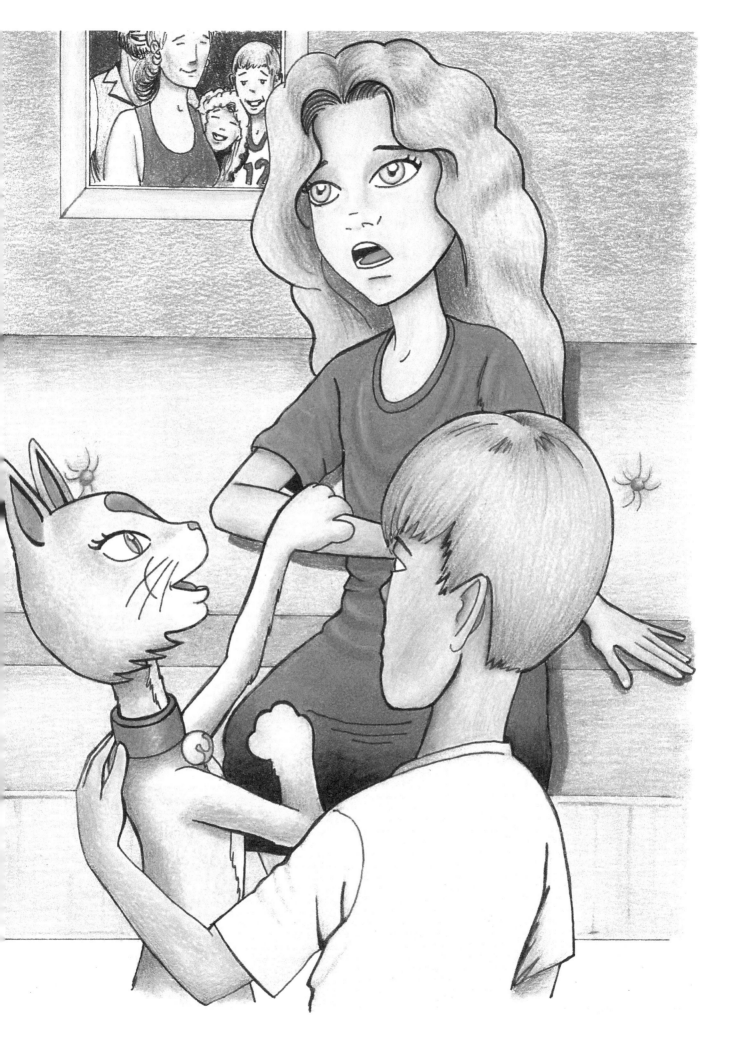

Matt and Dawn followed Love as she returned to the door.

Love walked with the children quickly thru the open door and back to Peace and the injured bird.

Peace, standing by the bush, looked at Love and winked, as if to say, "Nice job."

Matt moved to where the sound was in the bush. Dawn and Matt peered into that place in the bush.

Matt said to Dawn, "Oh it is a bird. It is hurt and unable to free itself. Dawn, go get a box. I will put the bird in the box."

Dawn left and returned with a big square, cardboard box. The box held a towel in the bottom of it. Matt very carefully put his hands on the injured bird, securely holding it and placing it into the box. Peace and Love were grateful that Dawn and Matt had so quickly gotten the mourning dove out of its prison, the bush, and into the shelter of the box. Now, they could see that the injuries of the bird were great.

Matt looking at the bird saw that one side of the bird; its wing and leg had been injured. Matt said to Dawn, "It looks like a bigger animal took this bird to a near end of its life!"

Peace and Love looked at one another and then glared in thought of what they had seen yesterday. The neighbor had a hunting dog. They had watched the man next-door work with the dog, in the yard. It would point with its tail and lift its leg in the direction of the decoy that the man would set about the yard. The man would say, "Get em!"

When the man was not working with the dog, it would bark and scamper after the birds in the yard. Peace and Love did not want to feel angry or hateful of the tragic idea of this training. They knew it was the nature of the dog to seize and contain birds, and yet they had not seen it happen to this bird. "The important thing," Peace said to Love, "Is that the bird get healed." Love looked back lovingly to the mourning dove in the box.

Dawn and Matt were thinking of the next steps they needed to do about the injured bird. Dawn said to Matt, "We must get the bird some food and water." Matt said, "You do that, Dawn, and I will tell Mother and Father about the injured bird."

Peace and Love sat quietly thinking about the process of healing the bird would have to go through to get well. Love said to Peace, "I hope the bird can make the journey to recovery." Peace said, "Me too, Love, me too."

Soon, Mother, Father and the children walked out of the house carrying the box. As they were walking to the car, Mother said, "The Bird Sanctuary will care for the bird and help it with medicine to heal its injuries." Father said, "It is quite a drive to the Bird Sanctuary, so, we must hurry."

Dawn patted Love's head. Matt saluted Peace, as he did sometimes in hopes of reassuring and respecting the concerned animals.

As they drove off, Peace and Love smiled with positivity and knowing that they had done all they could to help and rescue the bird.

The End

POWER...
MANY WEAKENED BY
UNTRYING MEASURES.
SOME FUTILE TO THE POSSESSION.
RECOGNIZED AS THE
GOOD, THE OMNI
REJOICE IN THE WELCOMING.
CHANNEL TO CREATE SUCCESSES.
ANSWER THE CALLING.
ADMIT INTENTIONS.
LIVE IN THE STRENGTH.

Lightning Source UK Ltd.
Milton Keynes UK
UKHW050732061020
371049UK00008B/112